CW00847860

First published in 1996 by Sapling,
an imprint of Boxtree Ltd, Broadwall House,
21 Broadwall, London SE1 9PL
Copyright © Geoffrey Planer, 1996

10 9 8 7 6 5 4 3 2 1

Except for use in a review, no part of this book
may be reproduced, stored in a retrieval system
or transmitted in any form or by any means,
electronic, mechanical, photocopying, recording or
otherwise, without prior permission of the publisher.

Reproduction by SX Composing DTP
Printed and bound in Great Britain by Cambus Litho Ltd.

ISBN: 0 7522 2305 4

A CIP catalogue entry for this book
is available from the British Library.

MOUSE TALES

Father Christmas's
Silly Brother William

Geoffrey Planer

⊞ sapling

For Tom
(a very sensible brother)

*Mr Tail was late back home. He opened the
door quietly and crept into the living room.
He tiptoed across the room.
'Me, me, me, me!!' said Fiona and Charles
as they both pounced on him from behind
the sofa where they'd been hiding.
'My turn, my turn, my turn,' they said, pushing him
into the Favourite Chair and jumping on his lap.
'I mont one 'bout Chrisams pressies,' said Fiona.
'But it isn't Christmas time yet,' said Mr Tail.
'Still mont it.'
'Hmm,' said Mr Tail, looking through
the pile of books. 'Hmm ... here we are.'
363 brothers and sisters peeped out
from where they were hiding too.
Mr Tail began the story.*

Another Night,
Another Mouse,
Another Tale . . .

Father Christmas's
Silly Brother William

Not many people know that Father Christmas has a brother called William – William Peter Christmas. And he's always trying to help.

But he's usually rather silly. So usually
he doesn't help at all. And that's why
everyone calls him Father Christmas's
Silly Brother William or Silly Brother
William for short or SB William
for shortest.

Now as you can imagine
Father Christmas is
a pretty busy sort
of person. All
through the year
he's sorting out
the presents,
putting them in
different piles for different countries –

separate bundles
for boys and girls,

separate piles
for the older kids,

trying to make
sure that batteries
are included – all
that sort of thing.

He's usually worked out who needs
to get what by the time the summer
holidays come. Then the elves service
the sledge early autumn,

making sure that it's
flying properly, oiling
the reindeers' harness,
polishing the bells
and so on.

The present wrapping starts properly about November. And each year Father Christmas hopes that he doesn't get ill at the wrong time. There are always a lot of colds and 'flu around at Christmas.

However ...

... last year Father Christmas started
feeling a bit sniffly about the middle
of December. But he wouldn't take the
medicine the doctor gave him because
it tasted so horrible. And the cold didn't
go away; and he still wouldn't take the
medicine. He said he was too busy to stop
work. And the cold still didn't go away.

The elves told him to go to bed and they said that they could finish the present wrapping-up for him, but Father Christmas wouldn't listen.

And the cold didn't go away even more. On the night before Christmas the cold had turned to 'flu.

Father Christmas sneezed and sneezed;
then he wheezed and wheezed; then
he snuffled and he coughed and
he sniffled and then ...

... he just had to go to bed.

The elves didn't know what to do and the whole place was in a real state, when who should walk in but ...

... Father Christmas's Silly Brother William. 'No problem,' said William, as he tried on the famous red coat.

'William to the rescue,' he chuckled as he
loaded up the sleigh with the presents.

'I've always wanted to have a go
on this,' he added, as he harnessed
the reindeer to the sledge.
'Jingle bells, jingle bells ...' he sang
as he clicked the reins and started to
move down the snowy runway.

'SB William requesting permission to take off,' he giggled.

'5,4,3,2,1 ACTION!' he shouted and the sleigh lurched off up into the cold night air.

Sadly, SB William didn't have a clue how to fly a sledge at all; twenty penguins had to suddenly dive for cover as he nearly crashed into them.

William pulled the reins and the sleigh shot up towards the clouds. 'Oooo errrr!!' cried William as he flew upside down over southern Africa.

'Crikey!' he exclaimed as he somersaulted over Poland and 'EEEKK!' as he bumped up and down over Sweden and Norway.

Even the reindeer were worried.
He managed to get the right way up by
the time they were flying over Australia.
He had slowed down at Japan; and
when he got to India he was beginning
to enjoy himself.

He zigzagged around Canada and the USA,
went really low over Argentina,
bucked over Panama,

turned left and zoomed over Ireland,
then Britain, and then went once
round France

before he looped the loop over Holland, did a wheelie past Germany and swooped on Denmark.
'I think I'll try a slow roll over Russia,' he giggled.

SB William had a wonderful time. He was away for hours.

SB William arrived back home windswept.
But he was very pleased with
himself; and so were
the reindeer.

'Hello chaps;
it's easy peasy
when you get
the hang of it,'
laughed SB William
to the worried elves.
'BUT YOU FORGOT
THE PRESENTS!!'
shouted the elves.

William looked behind him. There,
still in the sacks, were all the presents!
Undelivered!

The elves ran up to Father Christmas's
bedroom and told him what had happened.
'You've just got to take your medicine
now,' they said, holding out the spoon
full of green, nasty liquid.

Father Christmas sat up in his bed,

he held his nose,
he closed his eyes,
he made a face.
He opened his
mouth and
swallowed the
medicine down.

'Yukkkkkk!!'
he said.
And then,
'Yukkity
yuk yuk!'

But it worked. He jumped up out of bed.
The elves clapped and whistled.

They gave
Father Christmas
a flask of hot tea
and each reindeer
an extra carrot.

And so, wearing two pairs of socks and
an extra warm vest, and just a little bit
late that year, Father Christmas took off
into the night sky as usual to deliver
all the presents to all the children
all over the world ...

... as usual.

'And did he get to my house alright?' asked Fiona.
'And he got to your house alright,' said Mr Tail.
'And did he give me my presents?'
'And he delivered your presents;
now off to bed,' said Mr Tail.
'And did his cold get better?'
'And his cold was quite better
the next day. Bed!' said Mr Tail.
'And was he cross with Silly
Brother William?' asked Fiona.
'And he wasn't too cross with SB William ...'
said Mr Tail, '... but I will be if you are not
in bed and fast asleep by the time I count
to ... one, ' said Mr Tail pouncing.
365 little Tails rushed upstairs
squeaking with excitement.